DIRT BIKE WORLD

Supercross

by Matt Doeden

Reading Consultant:
Barbara J. Fox
Reading Specialist
North Carolina State University

CAPSTONE PRESS
a capstone imprint

Blazers is published by Capstone Press,
1710 Roe Crest Drive, North Mankato, Minnesota 56003.
www.capstonepub.com

 Books published by Capstone Press are manufactured with paper
containing at least 10 percent post-consumer waste.

Library of Congress Cataloging-in-Publication Data
Doeden, Matt.
 Supercross / by Matt Doeden.
  p. cm.—(Blazers. dirt bike world.)
 Includes bibliographical references and index.
 Summary: "Describes the sport of supercross, including rules, course details, and stars of the
sport"—Provided by publisher.
 ISBN 978-1-4296-5020-5 (library binding)
 ISBN 978-1-4296-5631-3 (paperback)
 1. Supercross—Juvenile literature. I. Title. II. Series.
 GV1060.1455.D64 2011
 796.7'56—dc22   2010004168

Editorial Credits
Mandy Robbins, editor; Tracy Davies, designer; Laura Manthe, production specialist

**Capstone Press would like to thank Ken Glaser, Director of Special Projects for the Motorcycle
Safety Foundation in Irvine, California, for his expertise and assistance in making this book.**

Photo Credits
AP Images/Daytona Beach News–Journal/David Tucker, 23; Ted S. Warren, 25
CORBIS/NewSport/Erich Schlegel, 26, 28–29
Getty Images Inc./WireImage/Craig Durling, 15
Newscom, 11, 17, 18, 27, cover; ABACAPRESS.COM/Cameleon/Thierry Plessis, 9, 20;
    Icon SMI/Anthony Vasser Southcre, 21, 24; Icon SMI/Perry Knotts, 10; UPI Photo/
    Aaron Kehoe, 12–13
Shutterstock/Marcel Jancovic, back cover
Steve Bruhn, 5, 6, 7

Artistic Effects
Shutterstock/Irmak Akcadogan, Konstanttin, Nitipong Ballapavanich, oriontrail,

Table of Contents

chapter 1

Race to the Finish

The final supercross race of the 2006 American Motorcyclist Association (AMA) season was on. Ricky Carmichael and Chad Reed were tied for first in the season's title competition. James Stewart was close behind in third place.

Fact: The 2006 title chase was the tightest AMA Supercross title competition ever.

Stewart jumped out to an early lead. Carmichael was hot on his heels. Stewart crossed the finish line first. Carmichael came in second. But second place gave Carmichael enough points to win his fifth AMA Supercross title.

Ricky Carmichael (left) and James Stewart (right)

chapter 2

SX Basics

Few sports match the action of supercross, or SX. The sport grew out of **motocross**. SX tracks have tight turns and high jumps. Events are held inside arenas or stadiums.

Fact: The Superbowl of Motocross was an indoor motocross race held in 1972. People shortened the name to supercross.

motocross—a sport in which people race motorcycles outdoors on dirt tracks

SX riders soar off high dirt jumps. They bounce over sets of small bumps called **whoops**. And they speed around sloped corners called **berms**.

berm

whoops—low bumps that are close together on an SX track
berm—a banked turn or corner on a supercross track

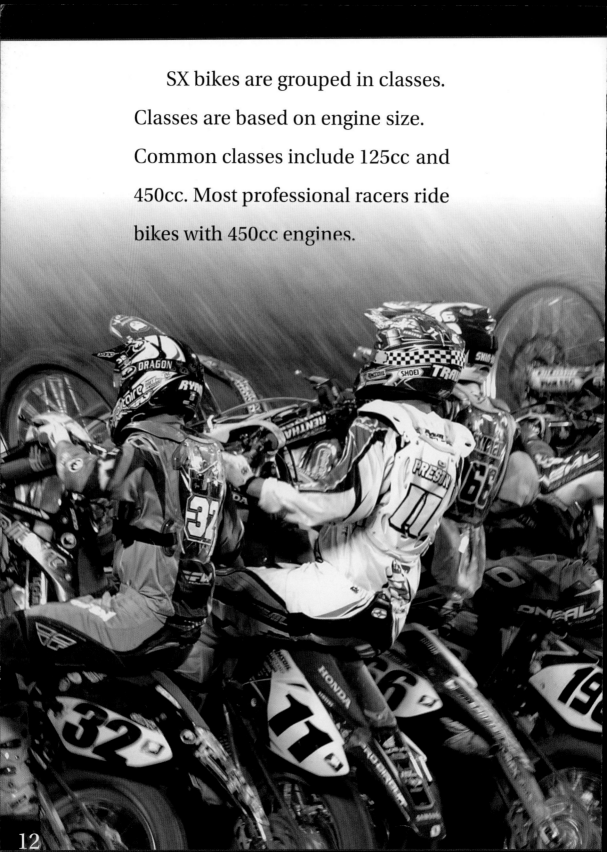

SX bikes are grouped in classes. Classes are based on engine size. Common classes include 125cc and 450cc. Most professional racers ride bikes with 450cc engines.

Fact: Engine size is measured in cubic centimeters. That's what "cc" stands for.

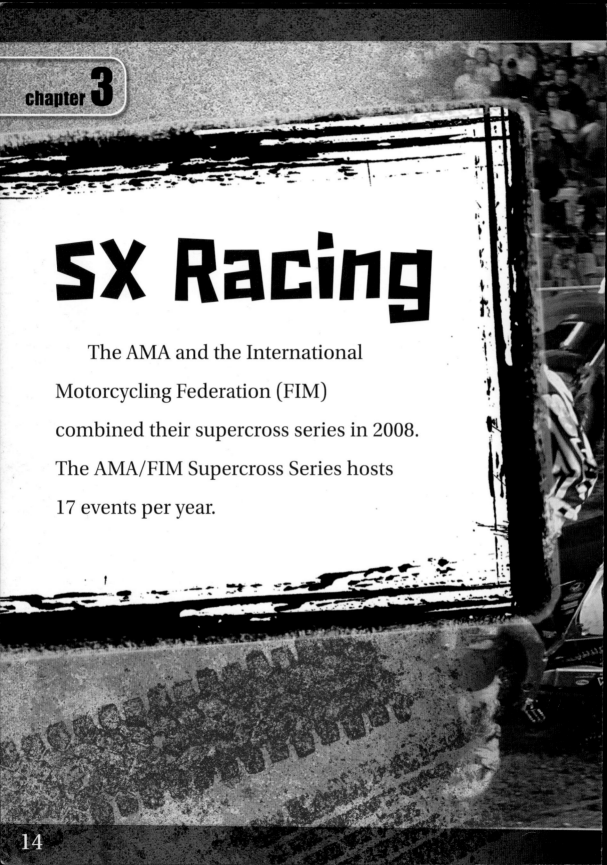

chapter 3

SX Racing

The AMA and the International Motorcycling Federation (FIM) combined their supercross series in 2008. The AMA/FIM Supercross Series hosts 17 events per year.

An SX event starts with two **heats**. The top nine riders from each heat advance to the main event. The other riders race in the last-chance qualifier. The top two riders from this race also compete in the main event.

heat—one of several early races that determine which riders advance to the main event

Fact: A maximum of 22 riders can compete in the last-chance qualifier.

Riders line up at the starting gate for the main event. The roar of 20 engines fills the air. Each rider wants to lead going into the first turn. This position is called the **holeshot**.

Fact: In the first AMA/FIM Supercross race of 2010, Ryan Dungey got the holeshot. He went on to win the race.

holeshot—the position held by the first rider through the first turn of an SX race

Riders push their bikes to the limit. They speed around tight corners and soar through the air. Some riders lose control and crash.

Fact: Most main event races last about 20 minutes.

chapter 4

SX Stars

Bob Hannah and Jeremy McGrath helped make SX popular. Hannah won three championships in the 1970s. In the 1990s, McGrath won four titles in a row.

James Stewart has been a force in SX since 2002. He has won three FIM Supercross Grand Prix titles. Stewart also earned two AMA Supercross Series championships.

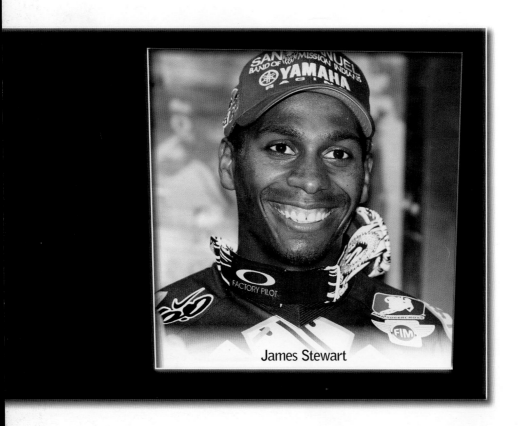

James Stewart

Fact: Fans call Stewart "Bubba." But his family's nickname for him is "Boogie."

Australian Chad Reed has won SX races and championships all over the world. He won the AMA championship in 2004 and 2008. Stars like Stewart and Reed keep fans coming back for more.

Chad Reed

Fact: In 2009, the AMA named Reed its Athlete of the Year.

Super Soaring!

Glossary

berm (BURM)—a banked turn or corner on an SX track

heat (HEET)—one of several early races that determine which drivers advance to the main event

holeshot (HOHL-shot)—the position held by the first rider through the first turn of an SX race

last-chance qualifier (LAST CHANSS KWAL-uh-fye-uhr)—a race held for riders who failed to qualify for the main event during the heat races; the top two finishers in the last-chance qualifier advance to the main event

motocross (MOH-toh-kross)—a sport in which people race motorcycles outdoors on dirt tracks

starting gate (STAR-ting GAYT)—a mechanical gate that drops at the start of a SX race; the starting gate ensures that all riders start at the same time

whoops (WOOPS)—low bumps that are close together on an MX or SX track

Read More

David, Jack. *Supercross Racing.* Torque: Action Sports. Minneapolis: Bellwether Media, 2009.

Levy, Janey. *Supercross.* Motocross. New York: PowerKids Press, 2007.

Mezzanotte, Jim. *Supercross.* Motorcycle Racing The Fast Track. Milwaukee: Gareth Stevens, 2006.

Internet Sites

FactHound offers a safe, fun way to find Internet sites related to this book. All of the sites on FactHound have been researched by our staff.

Here's all you do:

Visit *www.facthound.com*

FactHound will fetch the best sites for you!

Index